This book belongs to

_____

Published by Advance Publishers
© 1998 Disney Enterprises, Inc.
All rights reserved. Printed in the United States.
No part of this book may be reproduced or copied in any form
without the written permission of the copyright owner.

Written by Lisa Ann Marsoli
Illustrated by Dean Kleven, Phil Ortiz, Adam Devaney
Produced by Bumpy Slide Books

ISBN: 1-57973-012-4

10 9 8 7 6 5 4 3 2 1

Quasimodo greeted each new day with a smile. Now that he was free to roam outside the bell tower, he could see and do things he never imagined. Most of all, he enjoyed the company of his newfound friends.

He loved the hours he spent going on walks or picnics with Esmeralda, Phoebus, and Djali. And he especially delighted in helping Clopin put on puppet shows for the many children who lived in the town.

All the citizens of Paris were grateful to Quasimodo for ridding them of the evil Judge Frollo. It had taken a while for them to accept their new neighbor's unusual appearance. But the children became his friends right

away. Soon the grown-ups opened their hearts, too. Now when anyone — old, young, or in between — gazed at Quasimodo, all they saw was the kind and gentle man he was.

Quasimodo loved children and spent many happy hours among them. He made them special wooden toys. He told them stories and entertained them with Clopin's puppets.

And he always listened to what they had to say. When they were glad, he laughed along with them. When they were sad or frightened, he tried to comfort them. He didn't want any child to feel the loneliness he had felt during all his years in the bell tower.

One day, Quasimodo heard that a new family with two children had moved to town. He carved a horse for the boy and a cat for the girl. He did not want to go to their house uninvited, so he carried the toys in his pocket.

"I'm sure I'll run into them soon enough," he thought to himself.

And that's exactly what happened one beautiful morning as Quasimodo was talking with Esmeralda in the town square.

"Aren't those our new neighbors?" Quasimodo asked his friend.

"Yes," Esmeralda replied. "That's Madame and Monsieur Marceau, and their children, Madeline and Jacques."

When the wagon stopped and the family hopped down onto the cobblestones, Quasimodo and Esmeralda went over to introduce themselves.

"Hello!" Esmeralda called. "Welcome!"

"Thank you!" the father boomed back. "How kind of . . ." But he stopped speaking and his mouth dropped open in shock. Quasimodo was now close enough for him to see clearly.

"Children! Come at once!" cried the mother, grabbing each one by the hand. She thrust them behind her skirts.

Esmeralda pretended not to notice. She was used to people reacting to Quasimodo this way at first. "I'm Esmeralda, and this is my dear friend Quasimodo."

"Fine, fine!" the man mumbled brusquely. "Well, my family and I have shopping to do! Excuse us!" And the couple turned and quickly disappeared down the street with their children.

"How rude!" Esmeralda exclaimed angrily. She hated to see Quasimodo treated badly.

Quasimodo tried not to show it, but his feelings were hurt. "It's all right," he told Esmeralda. "I know how frightening I must look to them. There is plenty of time for us to get to know each other."

And then he placed the little wooden toys into
the back of the wagon where the children had been
sitting.

"What a good idea," Esmeralda said. "They are
sure to find them there."

A few days later, Quasimodo saw the children again. This time they were in the audience at one of Clopin's puppet shows. Their parents had left the youngsters to enjoy the performance while they attended to some business.

Madeline spotted Quasimodo behind Clopin's wagon and gave him a friendly wave. Then Jacques smiled and reached into his pocket. His hand came out clutching the wooden horse Quasimodo had carved for him.

After the performance, the children ran up to
Quasimodo to thank him for his gifts.

"I'm glad you like them," Quasimodo replied.

"We sure do!" Madeline replied. "How did you
know I love cats?"

"I didn't," Quasimodo told her. "But, you see, I
like cats, too. There are so many stray kittens here

in the city. I try to find homes for them whenever
I can."

"Maybe if you find another one, our mother and
father would let us keep it," said Jacques hopefully.

But before Quasimodo could answer, the children's
parents appeared.

"Madeline! Jacques! Get away from there! How many times have we told you not to talk to strangers?" the father scolded.

"He's not a stranger," Jacques protested. "He's our new friend, Quasimodo."

"The children and I were just talking," Quasimodo explained quietly. But the couple acted as if he were invisible. They bundled their children off to their wagon without another word.

Clopin saw what had happened and hurried over. "Come, my friend!" he said brightly, trying to cheer up Quasimodo. "We must get ready for the festival this weekend!"

The two went off to Clopin's wagon. Quasimodo carved new puppets while Clopin painted them and made costumes. As they chatted about the annual festival, Quasimodo's spirits lifted. Festival time was always exciting. Peddlers came from miles around and set up their stalls. Performers danced and sang,

acted and juggled on every street corner. Visitors poured into the streets to enjoy all the lively sights and sounds. And this year, Quasimodo would be helping Clopin create a brand-new puppet show.

When the day of the festival finally arrived, children crowded around Clopin's wagon. At the end of every performance, they clapped loudly and begged for more. The show was a huge success!

Jacques and Madeline couldn't wait to see the puppet show. They walked hand in hand behind their parents, hoping to reach Clopin's wagon in time for the next performance.

Suddenly a tiny calico kitten rushed in front of them. "Poor thing!" cried Madeline. "I'll bet it's lost!"

"Maybe we could get it something to eat," Jacques said. "It's awfully skinny."

"Here, kitty," Madeline cooed, bending to pick it up.

But the cat darted off. "C'mon!" Madeline called.
"It went this way!" The two children wove in and out
of the crowd. Then, all at once, the cat disappeared.
"Oh, no!" moaned Madeline. "I was hoping
Mother and Father would let us adopt it."

Jacques looked up at his big sister. "Where are Mother and Father?" he asked.

Madeline glanced around. "I'm sure they can't be far," she said, trying not to panic. Then she took her brother's hand and pulled him through the crowd. "Mother! Father!" she called.

For what seemed like a long time, the children searched the crowd for a familiar face. Every few minutes, Jacques's lower lip began to quiver. "Don't cry, now," Madeline said gently. "We'll find them."

Meanwhile, Clopin was closing up his puppet theater. "Time for a lunch break," he said to Quasimodo.

"Thank goodness!" Quasimodo laughed, picking up a prop. "I'm so hungry, even this wooden apple was beginning to look good!"

Quasimodo hurried to a food stall and bought some bread and cheese. Then he headed off to watch Esmeralda and Djali dance. But as he passed the cathedral, he saw two small figures crying in the doorway.

"Madeline! Jacques!" he called. "What happened?"

The relieved children ran to Quasimodo's arms and explained what had happened.

"You must have been so scared!" Quasimodo said sympathetically. "And I'll bet you're hungry, too!" He could see from the way the two gobbled up his bread and cheese that he was right!

Quasimodo lifted the children in his strong arms. "You'll be able to spot your folks better from up here," he told them. He began to walk slowly down the main street of the festival. Soon they reached the spot where Esmeralda and Djali had

just finished performing. Quasimodo was explaining to Esmeralda about the lost children when they heard frantic shouts.

"Stop! Kidnapper!" Monsieur and Madame Marceau shrieked as they confronted Quasimodo.

"Quasimodo found us," Madeline tried to explain. "He was bringing us back to you."

But her parents wouldn't listen to her explanation. They were calling for a soldier to arrest Quasimodo. Soon Phoebus came running.

"I know you must have been sick with worry," said Phoebus calmly. "But Quasimodo didn't kidnap your children."

"Of course he didn't," chimed in Esmeralda. "He was helping them find you!"

"The soldier is right, Mother," Jacques piped up. "Quasimodo is our friend. We've been trying to tell you."

The couple looked from their children to Quasimodo. The mother blushed and said, "I'm sorry we accused you. It's just that you are so . . . different. We didn't know what to think."

"You are right about one thing," Esmeralda said.

"Quasimodo is different. He is more kind and brave and loyal than any of us could ever hope to be."

"He is a dear friend to our children," said a woman in the crowd.

"When my barn burned down, he helped me rebuild it, stone by stone," a farmer added.

The father extended his hand. "Quasimodo, thank you for all you have done for my family. How can we ever repay you?"

Just then the calico kitten appeared and rubbed against Madeline's leg. "Well," said Quasimodo, "you can start by adopting that kitten!"

"What a wonderful idea," said the mother. She gazed warmly at Quasimodo. "It may be small and

skinny, but anyone can see it has a heart of gold."

The children cheered. "I know! Let's call it Lucky!" Jacques said.

"Perfect!" replied his father. "Because today we have been very lucky. Lucky to have found you and Madeline. Lucky to have found a new pet. And lucky to have made a new friend like Quasimodo."

Quasimodo's strange appearance
Often scared new folks away.
They turned their backs
And never heard
A word he had to say.
But the children only saw
The man he was inside —
A kind and gentle neighbor.
They called him "friend" with pride.